Friendship Club
El Club de la Amistad

Based on the episode "Cardboard Club" by Kris Marvin Hughes
Adapted by Gabrielle Reyes

Alma's Way © 2021, Think It Through Media, LLC.

All rights reserved. Published by Scholastic Inc., *Publishers since 1920.* SCHOLASTIC and associated logos are trademarks and/or registered trademarks of Scholastic Inc.

The publisher does not have any control over and does not assume any responsibility for author or third-party websites or their content.

No part of this publication may be reproduced, stored in a retrieval system, or transmitted in any form or by any means, electronic, mechanical, photocopying, recording, or otherwise, without written permission of the publisher. For information regarding permission, write to Scholastic Inc., Attention: Permissions Department, 557 Broadway, New York, NY 10012.

This book is a work of fiction. Names, characters, places, and incidents are either the product of the author's imagination or are used fictitiously, and any resemblance to actual persons, living or dead, business establishments, events, or locales is entirely coincidental.

ISBN 978-1-338-88314-5

10 9 8 7 6 5 4 3 2 1   23 24 25 26 27

Printed in the U.S.A.   40

First printing 2023

Book design by Ashley Vargas

Scholastic Inc.

Alma has a big surprise for her friends.

It's a giant cardboard box.

"We can make it into anything!" she says.

Alma tiene una gran sorpresa para sus amigos.

Es una caja de cartón gigante.

—¡Podemos convertirla en lo que queramos! —dice.

Rafia has an idea. "Let's make a clubhouse!"

Everyone agrees.

"First, we need to decorate it!" says André.

Rafia tiene una idea.

—¡Convirtámosla en un club!

Todos están de acuerdo.

—¡Primero tenemos que decorarla! —dice André.

Eddie joins the club. Everyone decorates the box.
Alma and Rafia draw a rainbow and flowers.

Eddie se une al club. Entre todos decoran la caja.
Alma y Rafia le dibujan un arcoíris y unas flores.

Then Alma and Eddie decorate the inside.
"This looks amazing!" says Alma.
"Fantastic!" says Eddie.
Luego Alma y Eddie decoran el interior.
—¡Se ve increíble! —dice Alma.
—¡Sensacional! —dice Eddie.

The friends love how their cardboard box looks.

"The Cardboard Club is now open!" Alma announces.

A los amigos les encanta como ha quedado la caja.

—¡El Club de Cartón abre sus puertas! —anuncia Alma.

Just then, Becka walks up to Alma.

"Cool cardboard box! Can I play too?" she asks.

En ese momento, Becka se acerca a Alma.

—¡Esa caja luce genial! ¿Puedo jugar yo también?

—pregunta.

"Sure! Everyone can play in our Cardboard Club!" says Alma.
"You're just in time for our first meeting. Everybody inside!"
—¡Claro! ¡Todos pueden jugar en nuestro Club de Cartón! —dice
Alma—. Llegas justo a tiempo para la primera reunión. ¡Entremos!

Everyone crawls inside the box. There isn't much space!
"Ouch! Someone is on my foot!" says Rafia.

Todos entran a gatas a la caja. ¡No hay mucho espacio!
—¡Ay! ¡Alguien se sentó en mi pie! —dice Rafia.

"Oof, someone's foot is on my head!" says Eddie.

—¡Uf, tengo un pie en la cabeza! —dice Eddie.

"Uh-oh," says Alma. "There's not enough room for all of us."

—Ay, no —dice Alma—. No hay suficiente espacio para todos.

Alma thinks. "I have an idea! When I need to fit all my toys in a box, I turn them in different directions. Let's give it a try. Rafia, turn to the back. Eddie, turn to the right!"

Alma piensa.

—¡Tengo una idea! Cuando tengo que meter todos mis juguetes en una caja, los pongo en diferentes direcciones. Intentémoslo. Rafia, voltéate hacia el fondo. ¡Eddie, voltéate a la derecha!

Alma crawls in. She squeezes past Becka.
She squishes between Eddie and Rafia.

Alma entra a gatas. Pasa junto a Becka.
Se aprieta entre Eddie y Rafia.

"Oof! There! Now we're all together," Alma says, "but we can't move . . . or play."

—¡Uf! ¡Ya está! Ahora cabemos todos —dice Alma—, pero no podemos movernos... ni jugar.

Alma isn't sure what to do next. Just then, Junior shows up.
"I love your cardboard box!" he says. "Can I play too?"
Alma no sabe qué hacer. En ese momento, aparece Junior.
—¡Me encanta esa caja! —dice—. ¿Puedo jugar yo también?

"The Cardboard Club is for everyone," says Alma.
"We have to fit Junior too. Everybody out! There's got to be a way!"
—El Club de Cartón es para todos —dice Alma—. Tenemos que lograr
que Junior quepa también. ¡Salgamos! ¡Tiene que haber una manera!

I gotta think about this . . .

Tengo que pensar...

What if we all take turns using the box? But then we wouldn't be together . . .

¿Y si nos turnamos para usar la caja? Aunque no estaríamos juntos...

What if we got a giant box big enough for everyone? But there's no way to get one box that big.

¿Y si conseguimos una caja lo suficientemente grande para todos? Aunque no es posible conseguir una caja tan grande.

"Wait, I know what to do!" Alma smiles. "I have a way we can all play together. But we're going to need a lot more boxes. Cardboard Club, are you ready for something BIG?"

—¡Esperen, ya sé! —sonríe Alma—. Se me ocurre una forma de que todos podamos jugar. Pero vamos a necesitar muchas más cajas. Club de Cartón, ¿están listos para algo GRANDE?

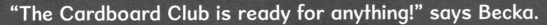

"The Cardboard Club is ready for anything!" says Becka.

"We won't leave anyone out!" says André.

"Let's do it!" says Junior.

—¡El Club de Cartón está listo para lo que sea! —dice Becka.

—¡Nadie se quedará fuera! —dice André.

—¡Hagámoslo! —dice Junior.

The friends collect boxes from all over the neighborhood.
They have lots of ideas. BIG ideas.

Los amigos recogen cajas por todo el barrio.
Tienen muchas ideas. GRANDES ideas.

After some hard work, they're ready.
"Welcome to Cardboard CITY!" says Alma.
Después de una ardua labor, la obra está lista.
—¡Bienvenidos a la CIUDAD de Cartón! —dice Alma.

There's a cardboard café, cardboard games, and even a cardboard garden!

¡Hay una cafetería de cartón, juegos de cartón y hasta un jardín de cartón!

"Great job, everyone!" Alma says with a giant grin.
"Hooray for Cardboard Club City!"
—¡Chicos, bien hecho! —dice Alma con una sonrisa enorme—.
¡Viva la Ciudad del Club de Cartón!

"There's room for everyone in Cardboard Club City," Junior says.
"Yup!" says Alma. "We can fit all our friends in Cardboard Club
City—as long as we have boxes. A LOT more boxes!"
—En la Ciudad del Club de Cartón hay sitio para todos —dice Junior.
—¡Sí! —dice Alma—. Todos nuestros amigos caben en la Ciudad del
Club de Cartón, siempre que tengamos cajas. ¡MUCHAS CAJAS!